I Wonder

I Wonder

Tana Hoban

Green Light Readers
Harcourt, Inc.
Orlando   Austin   New York   San Diego   Toronto   London

As I walk through the soft, green grass,
I wonder about all the animals I see.

A caterpillar bumps and inches along. Where did he come from? Where is he going?

A cobweb sparkles in the morning sun.
Who spun it? Is it hard to spin a web?

Little bugs zip back and forth. Are they happy or sad? Will they be glad when they get home?

A robin is sitting up on a branch. Is he getting set to fly away? Flying must be fun!

Who is that *buzz-buzz*ing from blossom to blossom? Something must smell sweet.

There's a zigzag track in the mud. Is this who came along with a wiggle and a jiggle to make it?

A plump frog is sitting at the pond. Will he jump in for a bath? I think he will.

A duck paddles along with ducklings. Are they all quacking at *me* as they swim by?

A kitten is playing in the grass. Is he out for a walk, just like me? I wish I could ask him.

As I walk back home, I wonder . . . Do all
the animals wonder about me?

Your Own Camera

Tana Hoban is a photographer.
You can be a photographer, too!

WHAT YOU'LL NEED

 paper tape

 crayons or markers

1 Fold a piece of paper in half. Tape the sides.

2 Make it look like a real camera.

3 Draw some pictures. Put them inside your camera.

4 "Develop" your film and share your pictures with your friends!

What Do You Wonder?

Make a list of things you see and wonder about every day.

I wonder about:

A New Story

Imagine what animals are wondering about when they see you. Write a story about it.

More About Animals

The animals that live around you are very interesting. See what you can find out about each of them. Share what you learn with a friend.

Meet the Author-Photographer

Tana Hoban takes a camera everywhere she goes. She is always looking for something new to take pictures of.

Tana Hoban took the pictures for *I Wonder* in Paris, France, where she lives. She hopes that they will help you see small things in a new way.

Copyright © 1999 by Harcourt, Inc.

www.HarcourtBooks.com

First Green Light Readers edition 1999
Green Light Readers is a trademark of Harcourt, Inc., registered in the United States of America and/or other jurisdictions.

The Library of Congress has cataloged an earlier edition as follows:
Hoban, Tana.
I wonder/Tana Hoban.
p. cm.
"Green Light Readers."
Summary: While walking through the park, a child sees a wondrous variety of animals.
[1. Animals—Fiction.] I. Title. II. Series.
PZ7.H638Iae 1999
[E]—dc21   98-55237
ISBN 0-15-204875-8
ISBN 0-15-204835-9 (pb)

A C E G H F D B
A C E G H F D B (pb)

Ages 5–7
Grades: 1–2
Guided Reading Level: H–I
Reading Recovery Level: 15–16

Green Light Readers
For the reader who's ready to GO!

"A must-have for any family with a beginning reader."—*Boston Sunday Herald*

"You can't go wrong with adding several copies of these terrific books to your beginning-to-read collection."—*School Library Journal*

"A winner for the beginner."—*Booklist*

Five Tips to Help Your Child Become a Great Reader

1. Get involved. Reading aloud to and with your child is just as important as encouraging your child to read independently.

2. Be curious. Ask questions about what your child is reading.

3. Make reading fun. Allow your child to pick books on subjects that interest her or him.

4. Words are everywhere—not just in books. Practice reading signs, packages, and cereal boxes with your child.

5. Set a good example. Make sure your child sees YOU reading.

Why Green Light Readers Is the Best Series for Your New Reader

● Created exclusively for beginning readers by some of the biggest and brightest names in children's books

● Reinforces the reading skills your child is learning in school

● Encourages children to read—and finish—books by themselves

● Offers extra enrichment through fun, age-appropriate activities unique to each story

● Incorporates characteristics of the Reading Recovery program used by educators

● Developed with Harcourt School Publishers and credentialed educational consultants

Daniel's Mystery Egg
Alma Flor Ada/G. Brian Karas

Animals on the Go
Jessica Brett/Richard Cowdrey

Marco's Run
Wesley Cartier/Reynold Ruffins

Digger Pig and the Turnip
Caron Lee Cohen/Christopher Denise

Tumbleweed Stew
Susan Stevens Crummel/Janet Stevens

The Chick That Wouldn't Hatch
Claire Daniel/Lisa Campbell Ernst

Splash!
Ariane Dewey/Jose Aruego

Get That Pest!
Erin Douglas/Wong Herbert Yee

Why the Frog Has Big Eyes
Betsy Franco/Joung Un Kim

I Wonder
Tana Hoban

A Bed Full of Cats
Holly Keller

The Fox and the Stork
Gerald McDermott

Boots for Beth
Alex Moran/Lisa Campbell Ernst

Catch Me If You Can!
Bernard Most

The Very Boastful Kangaroo
Bernard Most

Farmers Market
Carmen Parks/Edward Martinez

Shoe Town
Janet Stevens/Susan Stevens Crummel

The Enormous Turnip
Alexei Tolstoy/Scott Goto

Where Do Frogs Come From?
Alex Vern

The Purple Snerd
Rozanne Lanczak Williams/
Mary GrandPré

Look for more Green Light Readers wherever books are sold!